Monty Ahoy!

Colin West

Collins

Best Friends • Jessy and the Bridesmaid's Dress •
Jessy Runs Away • **Rachel Anderson**
Changing Charlie • Clogpots in Space • **Scoular Anderson**
Ernest the Heroic Lion-tamer • Ivana the Inventor • **Damon Burnard**
Two Hoots • **Helen Cresswell**
Magic Mash • Nina's Machines • **Peter Firmin**
Shadows on the Barn • **Sarah Garland**
Clever Trevor • The Mystery of Lydia Dustbin's Diamonds • Nora Bone •
Nora Bone and the Tooth Fairy • **Brough Girling**
Sharon and Darren • **Nigel Gray**
Thing-in-a-Box • Thing-on-Two-Legs • **Diana Hendry**
Desperate for a Dog • More Dog Trouble • **Rose Impey**
Georgie and the Dragon • Georgie and the Planet Raider • **Julia Jarman**
Cowardy Cowardy Cutlass • Cutlass Rules the Waves • Free With Every Pack •
Mo and the Mummy Case • The Fizziness Business • **Robin Kingsland**
And Pigs Might Fly! • Albertine, Goose Queen • Jigger's Day Off •
Martians at Mudpuddle Farm • Mossop's Last Chance •
Mum's the Word • **Michael Morpurgo**
Granny Grimm's Gruesome Glasses • **Jenny Nimmo**
Grubble Trouble • **Hilda Offen**
Hiccup Harry • Harry Moves House • Harry's Party • Harry the Superhero •
Harry with Spots On • **Chris Powling**
Grandad's Concrete Garden • **Shoo Rayner**
Rattle and Hum – Robot Detectives • **Frank Rodgers**
Our Toilet's Haunted • **John Talbot**
Pesters of the West • **Lisa Taylor**
Lost Property • **Pat Thomson**
Monty the Dog Who Wears Glasses • Monty Bites Back • Monty Ahoy! •
Monty Must Be Magic! • Monty – Up To His Neck in Trouble! • **Colin West**
Ging Gang Goolie, It's an Alien • **Bob Wilson**

First published in Great Britain by
A & C Black (Publishers) Ltd 1994
First published by Collins 1995
10   9   8   7   6   5

Collins is an imprint of HarperCollins Children's Books part of
HarperCollins Publishers Ltd. 77-85 Fulham Palace Road, London W6 8JB

ISBN 0-00-675004 4

Printed in Great Britain by
Clays Ltd, St Ives plc

Monty and the Model Boat

Simon, Josie and Monty, the dog who
wears glasses, were at the park.
They were trying out Simon's new
model boat on the lake.

Simon and Josie took turns at the radio controls to steer the boat.

It went this way

and it went that way

and it went this way again.

It was great fun for Simon and Josie, but Monty was rather bored.

Suddenly Monty felt a great
WHACK!

A football bounced off his head.

It landed in the boating lake with a
mighty splash.

A group of children came over to
Simon. They looked pretty cross.
The biggest boy stepped forward.

'Don't worry, I'll get your ball back,'
promised Simon.

Simon beat the water with a stick to try and move the ball towards him.

But it made matters worse, and the ball drifted to the middle of the lake. Now it was caught up in some weeds.

The gang were getting angry.
The leader eyed Simon's model boat.

Josie tried to think fast.
Hastily, she picked up Monty.

Josie carefully placed Monty on Simon's model boat.

Monty was so nervous he stood perfectly still so as not to rock about.

Then Josie took the controls and guided the boat towards the stranded football. Monty felt shaky at first. But before long he found his sea legs and began to enjoy the voyage.

Move over ducks, make way for Monty!

When Monty reached the ball, he
realised what he had to do. He
nudged the ball with his nose till it
was free from the weeds.

Then Josie guided the boat safely
back to shore, with Monty nudging
the ball all the way.

Josie plucked the football from the water and handed it to the leader of the gang.

Simon picked up Monty. 'You really saved the day,' he whispered.

I'm an old sea dog at heart!

Monty's Mixed-up Morning

Granny Sprod had come to stay for the weekend. Monty really liked Granny, but she *did* like playing energetic games rather a lot.

Come on Monty, stretch those little legs!

Hang on, Granny!

On Saturday morning, Granny Sprod was in the back garden with Monty. She was showing him how to do cartwheels.

Monty tried as well.

But he wasn't too good at them.

When Granny and Monty tried to do cartwheels together, they bumped into each other.

And both of them lost their glasses.

Granny Sprod fumbled around in
the flower bed for her glasses.

Ah! Here
they are.

Then she found Monty's glasses and
perched them on his nose.

It's lucky
nothing's broken.

Granny hadn't noticed that she'd got the glasses muddled up. Everything that Granny saw now looked much smaller.

And everything that Monty saw now looked **much larger**.

Just then Monty heard a flapping
sound. He looked up and saw a
blackbird as big as a vulture.
He disappeared indoors double
quick!

Granny couldn't understand why
Monty was so frightened of such a
tiny bird!

Granny Sprod followed Monty indoors. Lunch was just being served. Mrs Sprod handed Granny a plateful of food. But her meal looked really tiny to her.

Monty looked at the dinner which Josie had served him.

It looked really big to him.

Granny asked for second helpings
of everything.

But poor Monty felt he'd burst if he
ate much more.

Monty left half of his dinner.

Mrs Sprod was most concerned.
She took Mr Sprod aside.

Mr and Mrs Sprod began to argue.
And soon Simon began to quarrel
with Josie.

There was quite a rumpus going on.
Granny decided to get away from it
all.

Granny sat in her favourite
armchair and picked up the
newspaper.

Granny decided to have a nap
instead, and Monty soon joined her.

As Granny nodded off, her glasses
slowly slipped down her nose . . .

Bit by bit, they slid down until they
slid off the end of her nose.

They landed on Monty and knocked
off the glasses he was wearing!

Monty woke up with a start, and
Granny Sprod woke up too.

Granny rubbed her eyes and
fumbled around for her glasses.
This time she found the right pair.

Then Granny found Monty's glasses
and put them on his nose.

Now everything was back to
normal. And no one ever knew
what had really happened on that
mixed-up muddled-up morning!

Monty on Sports Day

It was Sports Day at Simon and Josie's school. Josie was to run in the final event, the Grand Relay. Simon had come to cheer her along.

Simon warned Monty to keep out of
Mrs Prendlethorpe's way. (She was
the Head Teacher and she didn't
like Monty one little bit!)

Monty behaved himself all
afternoon. He watched children
jumping high, children jumping
long and children jumping over
hurdles.

It was all very exciting, but Monty was glad when it was time for the final event – the Grand Relay.

Josie's team (in blue) had to beat the Red Team, the Yellow Team and the Green Team.

May the best team win – preferably the Blues!

One runner from each team lined
up at the start.
Mrs Prendlethorpe set them off.

On your marks,
get set, GO!

Everyone cheered as the runners
raced around the track.

Mrs Prendlethorpe gave a running commentary over the loudspeaker:

Monty was horrified! The boy who was passing the baton to Josie had gone and dropped it! Quick as a flash Monty bounded on to the track.

Before Josie could pick up the
baton, Monty gripped it in his teeth
and raced after the others.

Monty overtook the green runner,

and he overtook the yellow runner,

and he overtook the red runner.

Everyone cheered as Monty passed the finishing post. The Blue Team had won the relay!

But Mrs Prendlethorpe was livid.

Everyone was sad to hear the Head Teacher's decision. Even the other runners thought Monty deserved to win after his amazing feat.

But then Simon asked a question.

Mrs Prendlethorpe was lost for words.

Mrs Prendlethorpe looked through the Rule Book very carefully. In the end she had to admit she *couldn't* find any rules about dogs not competing.

So very reluctantly, she agreed to
let the result stand.

A loud cheer went up.
Monty was the star of Sports Day.

Mrs Prendlethorpe had to present
Monty and the rest of the Blue
Team with a silver cup.

But later, when everyone had gone
home, Mrs Prendlethorpe added a
new rule to the book.

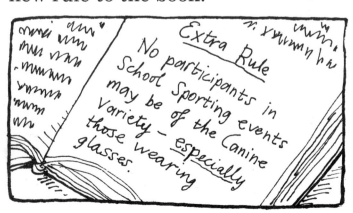

Monty and the Dog Food

One morning, Simon, Josie and
Monty were watching television.
During a break, there was a
commercial for a new dog food.

But Monty didn't like the look of it.

The advert went on . . .

But Simon and Josie had been won over.

Josie and Simon told their mum all about Chubby Chunks.

It's new!

It looks nutritious!

It seems good value!

Oh really? Then I'll get some this afternoon.

But Monty had other ideas.
He made a sick-looking face.

No one took any notice. How could
Monty tell them he didn't want
Chubby Chunks? He sat by the TV
and waited for the advert to appear
again.

WELCOME
TO
DAYTIME
T.V.

Monty had to sit through a silly
cartoon . . .

. . . a news bulletin . . .

. . . and an old film.

At last the Chubby Chunks
commercial appeared. 'Hooray!'
thought Monty. He barked loudly to
attract Simon and Josie.

But they got the wrong message.

Oh, no! Monty's plan had failed.

Monty moped around all morning.
His worst fears were confirmed
when he spotted Mrs Sprod's
shopping list.

Then Monty had another idea:
he could chew off the bottom bit of
the shopping list, and Mrs Sprod
would forget all about buying
Chubby Chunks!

So when no one was around, Monty took the shopping list and started chewing off the bottom part.

But all of a sudden Josie walked in.

Mum! Monty's so hungry he's eating the shopping list!

Another of Monty's plans had back-fired.

Now Monty was *really* miserable.
He wasn't looking forward to a diet
of Chubby Chunks.

He was sorry to see Mrs Sprod
leaving for the shops.

Monty moped around more
miserable than ever.

After a long while, Monty heard
Mrs Sprod come home again.

Monty noticed that Mrs Sprod
looked almost as sad as himself.

I'm sorry Monty, but all the shops have sold out of Chubby Chunks!

Monty perked up, and wagged his
tail joyfully.

Why Monty! Anyone would think you never wanted Chubby Chunks!

That evening, on TV, the Chubby Chunks advert came on again. Monty took another look.

'It really doesn't look too bad,' he thought.

But how could Monty get some? All the shops had sold out. Monty's life was full of problems!

Monty's New Year

It was the first day of the year.
Simon, Josie and Monty were
having fun in the snow. They built a
snowman, threw lots of snowballs
and took turns on the sledge.

Then they decided to take their
sledge to the very top of the hill.

They
　　zoomed
　　　　down
　　　　　　the
　　　　　　　　hillside
　　　　　　　　　really
　　　　　　　　　　　fast . . .

Everything was great until . . .

The sledge hit an old tree stump, and Simon and Josie were thrown off. Luckily they weren't hurt.

But Monty was flung through the air.

He crash-landed in a bed of soft snow.

Monty was stuck fast!
He couldn't bark, he couldn't yelp.
All he could do was waggle his legs
furiously.

Simon and Josie picked themselves up. They couldn't hear Monty's bark anywhere, and it was some while before they spotted his hind quarters.

Josie and Simon rushed over to
Monty and took a hind leg each.
Gently they pulled Monty free.

Monty was unhurt, but he *was*
frozen stiff, and his teeth were
chattering.

Simon put Monty under his arm
and headed for home.

Josie stood Monty in front of the fire to thaw out. He took longer to defrost than the Christmas turkey!